Cupcake Diaries
the new batch

Natalie's Double Trouble

By Coco Simon
author of Cupcake Diaries

Illustrated by Manuela López

Simon Spotlight
New York   London   Toronto   Sydney   New Delhi

SIMON SPOTLIGHT
An imprint of Simon & Schuster Children's Publishing Division
1230 Avenue of the Americas, New York, New York 10020
This Simon Spotlight edition June 2024
Copyright © 2024 by Simon & Schuster, LLC
All rights reserved, including the right of reproduction in whole or in part in any form.
SIMON SPOTLIGHT and colophon are registered trademarks of Simon & Schuster, LLC.
Simon & Schuster: Celebrating 100 Years of Publishing in 2024
For information about special discounts for bulk purchases, please contact
Simon & Schuster Special Sales at 1-866-506-1949 or business@simonandschuster.com.
Text by medina
Designed by Brittany Fetcho
Illustrations by Manuela López
The illustrations for this book were rendered digitally.
The text of this book was set in Bembo Std.
Manufactured in the United States of America 0424 MTN
2 4 6 8 10 9 7 5 3 1
Library of Congress Cataloging-in-Publication Data
Names: Simon, Coco, author. | López, Manuela, 1985– illustrator.
Title: Natalie's double trouble / by Coco Simon ; illustrated by Manuela López.
Description: Simon Spotlight edition. | New York : Simon Spotlight, 2024. | Series:
Cupcake diaries: the new batch ; book 2 | Audience: Ages 5 to 9. | Summary: Natalie
navigates responsibility and jealousy when she overcommits the Mini Cupcake Club,
leaving her twin sister Stephanie to save the day.
Identifiers: LCCN 2023041064 (print) | LCCN 2023041065 (ebook) |
ISBN 9781665952378 (paperback) | ISBN 9781665952385 (hardcover) |
ISBN 9781665952392 (ebook)
Subjects: CYAC: Twins—Fiction. | Sisters—Fiction. | Baking—Fiction. |
Responsibility—Fiction. | Jealousy—Fiction. | BISAC: JUVENILE FICTION /
Family / Siblings | JUVENILE FICTION / Cooking & Food
Classification: LCC PZ7.S60357 Nat 2024 (print) | LCC PZ7.S60357 (ebook) | DDC
[Fic]—dc23
LC record available at https://lccn.loc.gov/2023041064
LC ebook record available at https://lccn.loc.gov/2023041065

CONTENTS

Chapter 1: We Will, We Will Bake You!   1

Chapter 2: Pass the Cupcake   9

Chapter 3: The Cupcake Equation   17

Chapter 4: All Twins Considered   39

Chapter 5: Life Is What You Bake It   45

Chapter 6: Home Is Where the Twin Is   55

Chapter 7: Keeping It Acute   69

Chapter 8: Put a Little Cupcake
        in Your Heart   79

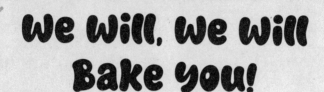

Chapter 1

We Will, We Will Bake You!

"Now that we're officially a club, we need to start brainstorming other events to bake for. We must keep our business going!" Alana said, pushing her glasses up and pulling out her calculator.

All the members of our new Mini Cupcake Club were sitting down for lunch on Thursday. I knew my friends were a little bit nervous. At the recent baking competition at our school, our submission in the cupcakes category had been named the best overall, but we were nowhere near being experts.

"You are always keeping on top of things, Alana!" I said, taking a huge bite of my *abuela*'s arroz con pollo (that's Spanish for "chicken and rice"). "You know . . . I think it would be super cool if we made mini cupcakes for some special events next weekend. Emily, we have our last soccer game of the season next Saturday, and, Ethan, your first basketball game is that Sunday, right?"

Ethan nodded. "Yeah. I really hope we win and start the season off right!"

"It's a great idea, Natalie, but do you think we should commit to baking so much so soon?" Ren asked hesitantly.

"Of course!" I said excitedly. "Ethan," I said, turning toward him, "tell everyone about the fabulous cupcake idea you mentioned to me!"

"Wait, what?" Ethan looked confused.

"You know . . . the idea you were telling me about yesterday! The really cute soccer cupcakes that have designs on them," I said, smiling at him.

"Oh, yeah . . . I think it could be cool to have the cupcakes we bake for the soccer game have a soccer ball frosting design."

Alana looked at Ethan. "That's a great idea! And then we could decorate the cupcakes for the basketball game with a basketball design."

"Wait, you just got me thinking," Ren said. "What if we made the actual cupcakes the shape of the basketballs?"

"That's an awesome idea," I said. *Our mini cupcakes are going to be amazing,* I thought. *We are going to be famous!*

Chapter 2

Pass the Cupcake

So, if you hadn't noticed yet, I'm pretty good at making sure everyone feels included and important. What can I say? I'm a theater kid! Everyone plays an important role!

On my way to theater club after school that same day, Emily stopped me in the hall. "I'm not sure if I really have anything special to offer to our cupcake club," Emily said, doubting herself.

"Don't worry," I reassured her. "Don't forget that baking cupcakes was your idea. You're the founder of the club, Emily!"

"Hmm . . . But what can I do now? What can I specialize in? I don't want to disappoint everyone." Emily nervously bounced her soccer ball off her knees.

"That's impossible! You're not going to disappoint anyone," I said, rushing off down the hall to theater club.

After rehearsal for our upcoming school play, my friend Nancy came up to me. "Natalie, I heard you and your friends won the award for the best overall cupcakes in the baking contest. Way to go!"

"Thanks," I replied. "We actually formed our own club. You know Ethan Moore? He's the one who made the pizza cupcakes for the contest. Well, he's baking with us now too!"

"Wow, that's so cool, Nat!" said Nancy. "Hey, maybe your club could make mini cupcakes for refreshments on opening night."

"Next Friday? Of course, no problem!" I agreed quickly. I couldn't wait to tell the rest of the club!

After theater club was soccer practice. When I met up with Emily on the field, I told her the good news. "Isn't it great?" I said proudly.

I was surprised at Emily's reaction. Instead of looking happy or excited, she looked a little bit scared. "I'm getting worried we won't have enough time to get all these orders done," she said.

"I'm sorry I didn't wait," I responded. "But the people have spoken, and they want cupcakes!"

While we were doing our dribbling and passing exercises, I thought about what Emily had said. *Emily just has to start thinking BIG!* I thought.

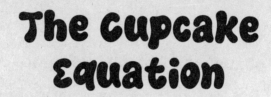

Chapter 3

The Cupcake Equation

The weekend went by in a blur. On Saturday morning, as my dad was making me breakfast, I stood up and started acting out my part for him. "Wonderful, *hija*," he said. "Now please sit down and eat. Your *huevos* are getting cold." He pointed to the untouched plate of scrambled eggs in front of me.

"Why don't you practice your lines with Stephanie?" my mom asked. She laughed. "I remember all the shows the two of you used to perform for us when you were little."

I shrugged. "Stephanie's too busy working on stuff for her math club," I said. I rolled my eyes. "She's all about the numbers."

My dad sat down next to my mom with a mug of coffee. "I miss when you two used to do things together," he said. "For a pair of twins, you aren't very twinlike anymore."

He was right. Even though we were identical twins, I couldn't remember the last time Stephanie and I did anything together.

As Emily and I walked to lunch together on Monday, she said, "I'm still nervous about the theater club order, Natalie."

I put my hand on her shoulder. "I'm telling you, everything's going to be fine."

I decided to announce my big news slowly. "So," I said, looking around the table to make sure I had everyone's attention, "you know how important it is to support all our fellow students equally, right?"

"Yes . . . ," Ren said hesitantly, tilting her head.

"I booked us to make two hundred mini cupcakes for the theater club's opening night this Friday," I said. Instead of looking happy, everyone had that same sort of worried expression Emily had when I first told her about the order.

"*Two hundred* cupcakes? My hands are tired just *thinking* about all that decorating!" Ren moaned.

"Why don't we just wait until the spring play, Natalie?" Alana suggested.

"Just picture it," I said in my most convincing voice. "Popcorn-flavored cupcakes for opening night!"

"I don't know if it's even possible to make that many cupcakes in such a short amount of time," Emily said.

"Let's talk more about this after school," I replied. "We can meet at my place. I'll catch up with Ethan and tell him to come over too." I gave Emily a bright smile even though I was starting to feel a little nervous myself. "You'll see my vision in no time!"

As I waited for my friends to arrive, I sat in the kitchen looking over my calendar for the week. *Maybe everyone's right,* I thought. *Maybe baking for three events in one week is just too much.*

As I sat there frowning, my twin sister walked in. "What's wrong, *hermanita*?" Stephanie passed me an orange juice and sat next to me. "You look a little upset."

The last thing I wanted was to let my sister know I'd messed up.

"Everything's fine," I said, taking a sip of the juice.

Stephanie pushed her chair out and started to get up. "Okay, just trying to help."

The doorbell rang, and Stephanie went to open the front door. "You have visitors, Natalie!"

"Hi, Stephanie. Are you going to stick around and help us?" Emily asked.

"Nope, Natalie doesn't want me to help," Stephanie replied. "So I'm just going to finish my homework."

I rushed to the front door. "Thanks for coming, everyone," I said. As we all settled into various chairs in the kitchen, I continued. "I've been trying to come up with a solution."

"Our schedules are so busy," Ren said. "I don't think we'd have time to decorate everything in just a couple hours."

"Maybe you're all right. This is a lot," I said. I felt like I was disappointing everyone: the soccer team, the basketball team, the theater club, and now my cupcake club members, too.

As my thoughts kept racing, I saw my sister coming back down the stairs.

"Just coming down to grab a little snack," Stephanie said to everyone as she headed toward the fridge.

"Hey, Stephanie. Natalie told me you're a math whiz. We could use your help," Alana said.

Alana told Stephanie about our big dilemma.

"Ah, I see. Well, why don't you have each member make a batch of cupcakes and then freeze them before frosting and decorating them. How many members are in your club?" Stephanie asked.

"Five, including me," Ethan replied.

I was a little uncomfortable that Stephanie was helping us, especially since she hasn't shown any interest in anything I've been involved in lately.

"Okay, if five members each bake forty cupcakes ahead of time and freeze them, you'll have the two hundred cupcakes for the night of the school play!" Stephanie suggested.

"But don't forget we also have to make cupcakes for the basketball and soccer teams," Emily said. "A hundred for each event."

"Right. So you just approach it the same way," Stephanie proposed. "You bake in numbered batches, maybe even in teams, freeze the batches as they're done, and then defrost them in plenty of time to decorate them."

"Let's make a schedule that spreads the baking out every night this week. I'll type it up on my tablet and message it to everyone," Alana offered.

I could see the relief on Emily's face. "Thanks so much, Alana, that sounds great."

"But . . . will freezing the cupcakes make them taste funny?" Ren asked.

"My sister does it all the time, and they taste fine!" Emily answered.

Everyone smiled and sighed happily. Emily's stepsister, Katie, started the Cupcake Club at her school, and now it was pretty famous in our town. So Emily knew what she was talking about.

I should have been grateful to my sister, but instead, I felt a little bit annoyed. And yes, a little bit jealous, too.

"What about *decorating* all those cupcakes, though? I promised top-notch designs!" I said a little louder than I'd intended.

Stephanie took out a pad of sticky notes and a pen from a kitchen drawer and started writing. "Yep, just what I had already calculated in my head. If each cupcake takes one minute to decorate, then you can decorate two hundred in just over three hours. If you start on the theater club order right after school on Friday, that should leave you plenty of time to decorate them before the show," Stephanie said.

"Wow, you really are a math whiz!" Alana was clearly impressed.

"And since there's no school on Saturday, we can start early that morning frosting the cupcakes for the soccer and basketball games for the weekend," Ethan chimed in. "Take care of that batch of two hundred in three hours or so too."

"I'll add it to the schedule!" Alana said happily.

"And we can keep the cupcakes at my dad's house," Emily added. "We have an extra freezer because my sister uses it for her club!"

"Okay, then everything's settled," I said. "Now we just have to choose what days we are all going to bake!"

Alana started taking notes on her tablet: Emily chose that very night to bake her forty for the theater club because she knew she already had all the ingredients at her house. On Tuesday, Ren and Alana would bake theirs together. On Wednesday, we'd all meet back at my house and bake cupcakes for the soccer and basketball games. On Thursday, Ethan and I would bake the rest for the theater club individually at our own houses.

Stephanie's plan was working. So why was I feeling so defeated?

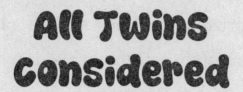

Chapter 4

All Twins Considered

The next day at lunch, my friends were going on about how great Stephanie was and how grateful they were to her.

"Don't you agree?" Alana asked, waving her hand in front of my face.

"Huh? What?" I had stopped paying attention a few minutes ago.

"I said, don't you think it's great that your sister helped us figure out how to make all the cupcakes in time?" Alana repeated her question happily.

"Yeah, sure. Listen, I have to memorize some lines for the play," I said, abruptly getting up and leaving.

Later, at soccer practice, Emily asked if I was okay. "Everything all right?"

"I feel like I didn't even get a chance to think of how to fix my mistake before my sister came swooping in to save the day," I admitted.

Emily nodded. "I totally get it. Sibling relationships can be hard. Are you two close?" she asked.

"We used to be close when we were little," I answered, "but now we have different interests."

"Maybe you two could talk it out," Emily suggested. "I know it always helps when I tell Katie how I'm feeling."

"I do miss spending time with Stephanie," I told Emily.

"I think you'll feel a lot better if you talk to her about what's bothering you," she said, giving me a quick hug.

I wasn't sure if or when I was going to bring up what I was feeling to Stephanie. But I was happy to know that I had a friend like Emily to talk to about stuff like this.

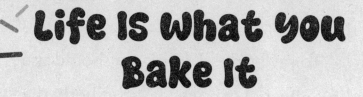

Chapter 5

Life Is What you Bake It

On Wednesday, everything was still going according to plan. Thanks to Stephanie, we already had one hundred twenty cupcakes baked, and Ethan and I would make the last eighty for Natalie's show tomorrow. At this pace, we'd have all the cupcakes ready for my show and the games this weekend. Tonight was our "group bake" for the sporting events, but we were just baking them and saving the decorating for Saturday morning, so we knew it would be a quick, worry-free night.

"To save time, I think we should use the same flavor cupcakes for both the soccer game and the basketball game," Ethan suggested.

"I agree!" Emily said, lifting her head from the baking tools she'd been arranging in perfect and logical order.

"Me too," I said. "Let's do chocolate for both. Chocolate will look good with the orange frosting when someone takes a bite out of a basketball cupcake, and it'll also look good with the white frosting on the soccer ball cupcakes."

"And, as promised, I brought my mother's cake pop molds and baking sheets!" Alana said, starting to empty the tote she'd brought along with her: five molds that made twenty mini cake rounds each and five metal sheets to bake them on.

"That's awesome! I love it!" Ren said.

Once all the equipment was spread out on the counter, we moved to the kitchen table to make sure that Ethan had all the ingredients ready for the batter. When he was done making it, we divided it into five separate bowls and each of us poured our share into our own cake pop mold atop our own baking sheet.

Just then my mom came into the kitchen. She had preheated the oven for us and was checking that it was now okay for us to start baking our cupcakes. She nodded to all of us. "Natalie and Emily, please do the honors!" Alana gestured to me to slide all the baking sheets into the oven, and Emily confidently set our timer for precisely fourteen minutes.

My mom smiled and said, "Everything looks good, *hija*. Remember to get me when you're ready to take the cupcakes out of the oven." I nodded and gave her a kiss on the cheek before she left.

While everyone was busy shuffling around the kitchen, my sister came in and just sort of quietly watched us.

"You're so organized," I heard her say to Emily.

"Gee, thanks," Emily replied. "I know my way around the kitchen thanks to my sister."

"Oh, really? Are you two close?" Stephanie asked.

"We are," Emily said.

"That sounds nice. I wish Natalie and I were still close." Stephanie sighed. I looked at her surprised. Did she realize I could hear what she was saying?

"Maybe you two should talk," Emily suggested, just as she had to me.

They both looked my way. I didn't know what to say to my own twin sister. The only thing I could think of was to make a joke instead. "Hey, we should make all our teachers apple-shaped cupcakes," I said, giggling.

"No more cupcake projects right now, Natalie!" Ren said with a laugh.

"Hey, at least I asked first this time!" I said, and then I laughed too.

Chapter 6

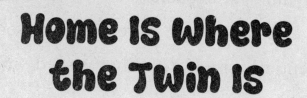

Home Is Where the Twin Is

It was great to see all the progress we'd made so far. Thursday was my day to bake forty cupcakes, and I was excited to head home and get started right away. As I was leaving school that afternoon, Emily stopped me and asked if I'd talked to my sister last night after everyone had left.

"No," I told her. "We were both tired. And I'm not sure what good it'll

do. We don't have anything in common anymore," I explained.

"It's okay to be different from your identical sister," Emily assured me. "Different is good."

"You do have a point. But we're not really identical. See?" I pointed to my chin. "I have a freckle on my chin and Stephanie doesn't." I giggled.

When I got home, Stephanie was already in the kitchen. She even had an apron on.

"Hi, twinsie!" she greeted me, and we both laughed. When we were in second grade, a couple of the "mean girls" in our class wanted to tease us. They started calling us "twinsies," thinking we'd hate it. Instead, we loved the nickname and called each other "twinsie" all the time.

"Nice apron, Steph," I joked.

"What can I say? I wanted to give you a hint . . . a big one!" Stephanie replied. She looked at me with a shy smile. "I'd really like to bake with you. I miss doing things with you."

I felt a wave of love for my sister rush over me. I had to ask her, just to be sure.

"Wait . . . you really want to help me bake mini cupcakes?"

"I thought you'd never ask!" she said.

"I want to have fun with you again," Stephanie said wistfully. "Remember when we were little and we'd do practically everything together?"

"Yeah, and we'd trick Abuelita all the time, and she'd get us mixed up," I added.

We both laughed.

"You know we can have our own interests and still do things together," I said.

"You're totally right. Let's start with baking!" Stephanie cheered.

"All right, just follow along with what I do," I told her. "We'll be done in no time!"

It was fun baking with my sister. I was in the middle of counting how many cupcakes we had cooling on the rack when she interrupted.

"Uh, sis?"

"Yeah?"

"I already counted," Stephanie said. "And . . . well . . . we made an extra forty by accident!"

I laughed. "That's because we were having so much fun together."

"Why don't you bring them to your opening night?" Stephanie suggested.

It was really nice of her to think of me, but I wanted her to know that I cared about her hobbies too. "Actually, I think you should bring them to your math competition tomorrow."

"Really? I didn't even think you knew about my competition. Thanks, *hermanita*!" Stephanie gave me a hug.

"It still feels weird," I said.

"The hugging? I know, it's like I'm hugging myself."

"Same here! I wonder if all twins feel like that."

"Do you know what I wonder? I wonder if all twins can bake as well as we can." Stephanie smiled.

I was glad I was finally able to talk with my sister. Hopefully, she knew how grateful I was to have her as a sister, a best friend, and a baking partner!

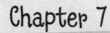

Chapter 7

Keeping It Acute

I woke up happy the next day, with a full heart. My sister and I had reconnected, and I had a busy, exciting Friday ahead of me.

"I hope you're up!" my dad hollered from the bottom of the stairs.

"Rise and shine, *hijitas*. Big day!" my mom added.

The school day zipped by, and afterward, everyone rushed to Emily's house to start decorating the cupcakes she'd pulled out of the freezer that morning before school. Everyone except me, that is. I'd decided to cheer Stephanie on at her math competition that afternoon instead of joining the decorating crew.

At first, I felt really torn about it, but when I'd told Emily at school, she'd assured me that it was fine and that she would cover for me with the club. Emily seemed really happy that Stephanie and I had bonded again, and it felt really nice to have such a caring friend.

I hurried home and grabbed the extra forty cupcakes. I wanted to surprise Stephanie with a cool design.

I'd decided to decorate each cupcake with different sorts of math symbols, in honor of Stephanie's competition. I used the leftover little tubes of writing icing to make number signs, division signs, pi, the square root symbol—everything I could think of!

I was done in under an hour, and before I knew it, it was time for my parents and me to head out.

"Watch out for the bumps. I'm carrying precious cargo," I told my parents from the back seat.

"You got it," Dad replied.

When I got to the library where the competition was, I took one last look at the cupcakes, making sure they were still perfect.

"Thanks to Dad's impeccable driving, there were zero casualties." I laughed and sat down in the first row with my parents.

Soon, Stephanie walked into the room with the rest of the Keeping It Acute math team at Fenton Street School, and I cheered and waved at her.

I watched her and her team do an amazing job for the first half of the competition and almost forgot I had to leave soon to get ready for the show.

"Nat!" Stephanie rushed over during the break. "Go, you don't want to be late!"

"Are you sure you don't need me here?"

"I'm sure! Now go!" My sister smiled at me as I ran from the library to the auditorium.

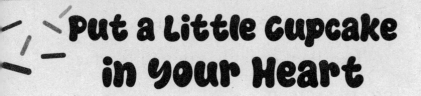

Chapter 8

Put a Little Cupcake in your Heart

It was almost showtime, and I had a few minutes to relax backstage in my costume. I felt like I hadn't had a second to myself all day. Suddenly, I had a call on my tablet. It was Emily video calling me from her tablet. She showed me that she, Ren, Alana, and Ethan were sitting in the audience, front and center, waiting for the play to begin.

"Your parents and Stephanie are

here too!" Emily said. She held up her tablet so I could see them. It was so good to see Stephanie there.

Then Ren quickly popped her face into the screen.

"Wait till you see the cupcakes, Nat!" she said. "They look amazing!"

"I can't wait!" I told her.

When the show ended, the cast all went out into the seated audience, and I thanked everyone for coming. The platters of mini cupcakes looked incredible. They all had vanilla frosting sprinkled with edible gold glitter, and each one had a tiny Tony

Award sticking out on top. (That's a big award given out in the theater world.) Ren had found bags of the tiny plastic trophies at a dollar store.

"We saved one just for you," Alana said, holding out her hand.

"Thanks," I said, devouring it in one bite.

"And before you ask," Stephanie said, "my team lost the math competition. But we looked acute doing it." Stephanie cracked up at her own goofy joke.

"I'm sure!" I said, smiling. "Thanks for all your help this week, Steph. And, Emily, thank *you*. If it wasn't for you, my sister and I wouldn't be where we are right now."

"That's true," Stephanie said. "We both wanted to be close again." She turned her face to me. "Right, twinsie?"

"Twinsies forever!" I said.

I took Emily's hand in mine. "I want to thank you again, Emily, for working your cupcake magic with me and Stephanie. It really made a difference."

"It's true," Ethan added. "We will never lose a baking tool or miss a baking beat with Emily taking care of things."

"Thank you all," Emily said quietly, shyly smiling.

I'm glad Emily could finally see her special place in the club.

"All right, all right, bring it in." Stephanie opened her arms and invited everyone in for a group hug.

Over the weekend, Ethan's basketball team won the first game of the season, and the mini cupcakes were a hit.

And even though our soccer team lost the last game of the season, we all felt like winners. Sports and theater shows were all well and good, but there was so much more to be happy about: we had our delicious mini cupcakes—and one another!

Still Hungry?

Here's a bite of the third book in the Cupcake Diaries:
The New Batch series, *Ren's One-of-a-Kind Cupcakes*

"Did everyone get a chance to take their turn during today's popcorn reading?" Mrs. Nelson scanned the room while everyone nodded yes, except for me. I love playing popcorn—but today I was skipped.

I just moved here and being in a new school filled with people who already know one another is really hard. And I can be kind of quiet until you get to know me, so it's a bit harder for me to make friends.

Rrriing!

The sound of the bell was music to my ears. It was lunchtime! As soon as I was in the hallway, I made a beeline for the cafeteria.

I felt pretty lonely when I first started attending Fenton Street School. But then I met Alana, Natalie, and Emily, and things have been great since then! We formed the Mini Cupcake Club, and we even won a baking competition with our first-ever entry.

Right before I made the final turn toward the cafeteria, I heard my name.

"Hey, Ren! Wait up!" I stopped in my tracks. I turned and saw Ethan.

"Hi, Ethan!" Ethan helps out with

the Mini Cupcake Club. Sometimes he gets wild ideas for cupcake flavors, but he's also a super hard worker and a lot of fun to be around.

As we headed to lunch together, we saw a colorful poster taped to the wall. KINDNESS WEEK was written on the top in big bold letters.

Ethan and I stopped to read it. We learned that next week, Fenton would be offering all kinds of activities to help us be kinder to one another.

As I read, I felt a flicker of excitement. "I wonder if we can make cupcakes for our classmates during Kindness Week?" I said to Ethan. "After all, what's kinder than a cupcake, right, Ethan?"

Ethan grinned. "I love it!"

We raced to the cafeteria. By the time Ethan and I got to our usual table, Alana was already there. Alana is our club's manager, which means she keeps track of our baking events.

"What's new, Ren?" she asked me.

"I've got an idea for Kindness Week!" I told Alana about making cupcakes for students.

"That's awesome!" Alana said. "Maybe we could make a different flavor for every activity. With a different design for each one too!"

I paused. This was *my* idea. I wanted

to be in charge of it and take the lead for once. "Maybe," I said, and then I turned to Ethan to change the subject. "Hey, you were amazing in the basketball game yesterday afternoon!"

For the rest of lunch, Ethan, Alana, and I talked about Ethan's winning basket. I thought I'd dodged Alana's ideas, but later that night she called me.

"What's up, Alana?"

"I've got it all planned out," she said.

"Alana!" I knew I said her name a little too loudly, but I was tired of feeling ignored. "I don't need your help. I just wanted to know if you liked the idea."

"Oh," Alana said. There was a pause.

"So . . . you don't want to hear what I came up with?"

"No. Ethan and I will handle everything," I blurted out.

"Well, fine," Alana said in a weird voice.

"See you tomorrow," I said, and we hung up.

I stood with the phone in my hand for a few seconds with a weird feeling I couldn't put my finger on. That was the shortest conversation I'd ever had with Alana.

The more I thought about it, the more I didn't want to discuss my idea with Emily and Natalie, either. I wanted to show everyone that Ethan and I could do this on our own.